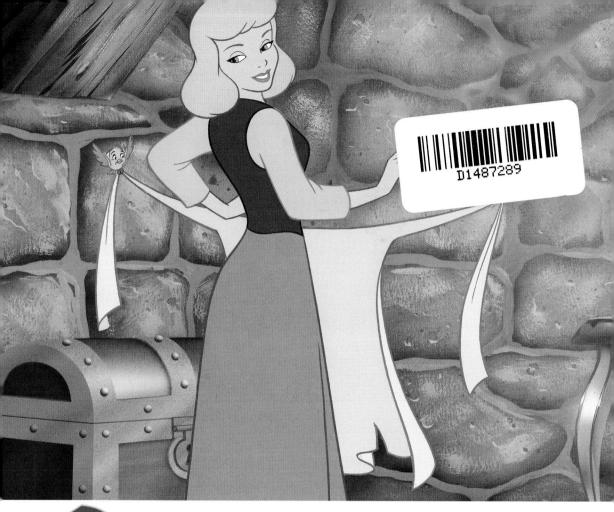

Once there was a kind and beautiful girl named Cinderella who lived with her cruel stepmother and two selfish stepsisters, Anastasia and Drizella. They made her slave all day, wear ragged clothes, and sleep in the attic. But Cinderella never complained. Every morning, she told her little mice and bird friends about her dreams.

"They're wishes my heart makes when I'm asleep. If I believe in them, someday they'll come true!"

Every day, from dawn to dusk, Cinderella's stepmother ordered her to work harder.

"Now, let me see, there's the large carpet in the main hall... clean it! And the windows upstairs and down... wash them! And don't forget the garden, then sweep the halls and the stairs... and there's the mending and the sewing and the laundry...."

"Yes, Stepmother."

But no matter how hard Cinderella worked, she never stopped dreaming.

Then one day, an announcement arrived from the palace. "The King is giving a Royal Ball in honor of the Prince. Every maiden in the kingdom is commanded to come!"

The stepsisters were thrilled, and so was Cinderella. "Every maiden! That means I can go, too!"

Her stepsisters laughed, but her stepmother smiled slyly. "You may go, Cinderella, if you do all your work. And if you find something suitable to wear!"

All that day, Cinderella's stepmother and stepsisters shouted orders at her. "Cinderella! Cinderella! Find my beads, curl my hair, iron our gowns and mend my sash!"

Cinderella's friends watched sadly. "Poor Cinderelly. They'll keep her so busy she'll never get her dress done." Then they had an idea! "We can do it! We can help our Cinderelly!" Soon, they were happily snipping and stitching to make a lovely dress for Cinderella.

When evening came, Cinderella trudged sadly up the stairs to her tiny attic room. "Oh well, what's a Royal Ball? I suppose it would be frightfully boring."

As she opened the door, her friends began to shout. "Surprise! Surprise!"

When she saw the pretty gown they had made for her, Cinderella could hardly speak. "Oh! How can I ever... oh, thank you so much!"

Cinderella ran downstairs. "Wait! Please! Wait for me!"

The stepsisters saw how lovely Cinderella looked and flew into a jealous tantrum and ripped her dress to tatters, while the stepmother watched with a nasty smile.

"That's enough girls. Don't upset yourselves before the ball. It's time to go."

Laughing cruelly, they left.

Cinderella was heartbroken. She ran into the garden weeping. "It's no use. There's nothing left to believe in!"

Suddenly, she heard a cheery voice. "Nonsense, child. If you didn't believe, I wouldn't be here... and here I am!"

Cinderella looked up and saw a plump old woman smiling at her. "I'm your Fairy Godmother. Dry your tears. We must hurry! First we need a pumpkin and some mice! Now for the magic words – Bibbidi-bobbidi-boo!" With a wave of her wand, the Fairy Godmother turned the pumpkin into a coach and the mice into white horses!

The Fairy Godmother hurried Cinderella to her coach. "But... but... my dress."

"Yes, yes... it's lovely — good heavens, child! You can't go in that. You need a dress!" Well, just leave it to me! What a gown this will be! Bibbidi-bobbidi-boo!"

She waved her wand, and Cinderella's rags changed into a shimmering gown. On her feet, two dainty glass slippers twinkled like stars.

"Oh, it's like a wonderful dream come true!"

But as Cinderella climbed into the coach, the Fairy Godmother gave her a warning. "Like all dreams, this can't last forever. On the stroke of twelve the spell will be broken, and everything will be as it was before."

"I understand. But it's more than I ever hoped for! Thank you!" She blew the Fairy Godmother a kiss and the coach sped away, carrying her toward the castle's shining lights and the Royal Ball.

Meanwhile at the ball, the Grand Duke and the King watched his son, the Prince, bow to one maiden after another with a polite but bored expression. "I can't understand it! There must be one girl who would make a suitable wife for a Prince!"

When Anastasia and Drizella curtsied before the Prince, they were so clumsy and giggly, that he could barely keep from yawning. Then suddenly, a hush fell over the ballroom.

The Prince looked toward the grand entrance. A lovely girl in a dress the color of moonlight stood there with all eyes on her. It was Cinderella, but her stepmother and stepsisters didn't recognize her. "Who is she, mother?"

"I don't know, but she seems familiar."

Prince Charming knew he'd found the girl of his dreams. He bowed to her. "May I have this dance?" As the music played, they began to waltz.

Around the ballroom they danced, past the delighted King and the Grand Duke. Past the jealous stepsisters and suspicious stepmother. On and on Cinderella and the Prince danced… out of the ballroom… and into the garden. Cinderella felt as if she was in a dream. But as she and the Prince sat beneath the starry sky, the castle clock began to chime.

"Oh my goodness! It's midnight! I must go! Goodbye!"

As Cinderella ran from the garden, the Prince rushed after her. "Wait! Come back! I don't even know your name!"

She darted through the ballroom and flew down the palace steps, losing a glass slipper on the stairs. The clock chimed on. Cinderella jumped into her coach, sped through the castle gates and raced down the road.

Suddenly, the spell ended. The coach became a pumpkin, the horses were mice, and Cinderella was dressed in rags again.

The next day, the King sent out a Royal Proclamation. "Every maiden in the kingdom must try on the glass slipper. And the girl whose foot fits will wed the Prince."

Cinderella couldn't hide her happiness from her stepmother. "So, Cinderella is the girl the Prince seeks. Well, he'll never find her!"

Quietly, she followed Cinderella to the attic, shoved her into her room and locked the door. "Please! You can't do this! Please, let me out!"

Ignoring Cinderella's cries, the stepmother went to the parlor where the Grand Duke and the footman were trying the slipper on Anastasia and Drizella. But though they pushed and shoved, the stepsisters couldn't jam their feet into it. "I don't understand why! It always fit perfectly before!"

Meanwhile, the mice grabbed the key and lugged it upstairs. "Thissa way. Up, up, up wif it. Gotta hurry!" They slid it beneath Cinderella's door. She was free!

The Grand Duke knew neither stepsister was the girl he sought. "Are there any other maidens in the household?"

"There is no one else, Your Grace."

Just as he turned to leave, Cinderella ran downstairs.

"Your Grace! Your Grace! May I try it on?"

The stepmother and stepsisters were furious.

"Ridiculous! Impossible! Pay no attention to her. She's only our scullery maid from the kitchen."

But the Grand Duke saw that Cinderella was lovely despite her ragged clothes. "Madame, my orders were to try the slipper on every maiden."

But as the footman carried the slipper to Cinderella, the stepmother tripped him, and he fell! The slipper flew up – and smashed into a hundred pieces on the floor.

The Grand Duke was horrified! "Oh no! This is...
this is terrible! What will the King say? What will he
do?"

Cinderella smiled and reached into her apron pocket.
"Perhaps I can help. You see, I have the other
slipper."

The stepmother and stepsisters gasped as Cinderella
pulled out the other slipper and handed it to the
Grand Duke. With a low bow, he slipped it onto her
dainty foot. And it fit perfectly!

Soon, wedding bells rang throughout the kingdom. With her little friends by her side, Cinderella married the Prince. And as they rode away in the Royal Coach Cinderella knew it was true. If you keep on believing, the dreams that you wish will come true.

And so they all lived happily ever after together.